Dedicated to all children who
enjoy a good adventure!

www.mascotbooks.com

The Ruth Adventures: Best Friends Forever

For more information, please contact:
Mascot Books
620 Herndon Parkway, Suite 320
Herndon, VA 20170
info@mascotbooks.com

Library of Congress Control Number: 2020909296

CPSIA Code: PRT1120A
ISBN-13: 978-1-64543-526-6

Printed in the United States

THE RUTH ADVENTURES

BEST FRIENDS FOREVER

Nancy Youngdahl

Illustrated by Diana Delosh

Ruth lives with her family on a small rural farm in North Carolina. Summer is over and it is time for school to start. Ruth had been homeschooled through first grade, but Ruth's mama wants to go back to work teaching fourth grade again.

Over the summer, Ruth's parents decided they wanted her to attend River's Edge Elementary School in town where Mama would be teaching. Ruth was excited, but also a bit anxious to start school. But, Ruth knew she would be able to see Mama during the day. Mama and Daddy told Ruth she would meet lots of new friends at school.

Being in the country and away from the town center, she had few friends that were her age to play with. Now Ruth would be able to invite new friends to visit her, and even have sleepovers on the weekends!

The first day of school arrived, and Ruth rode to town with Mama. On the way there, Mama said to Ruth, "Always pay attention to the teacher and don't talk when your teacher is speaking to the class."

Mrs. Sloan

When they arrived at the school, Mama took Ruth to her second-grade classroom and introduced her to Mrs. Sloan, Ruth's teacher for the school year.

Because Ruth was a bit early, there was only one other girl in the classroom. Her name was Sue. Being friendly, Sue went over to Ruth's desk and said, "I'm Sue, are you a new student here?"

"Yes, I am," said Ruth.

Sue replied, "Well, this will be my third year at River's Edge, and if Mrs. Sloan will let me, I'd like to show you around the school."

M rs. Sloan said that would be okay, so off they went down the hall to check out the other classrooms on the first floor.

River's Edge Elementary School was an old, three-story building. Ruth's mama's classroom was on the second floor where all the bigger kids were, so they didn't visit her class. Sue also showed Ruth the playground, and they played on the swings. When the school bell rang, Sue and Ruth went back to their classroom. Several more children had arrived, and Sue introduced Ruth to them.

At lunch time, Ruth, Sue, and several other girls and boys ate together, and then went out to the playground.

The girls jumped rope together and then played hopscotch as the boys played baseball. By the end of that first day, Ruth had a new friend, and her name was Sue.

On the ride home with Mama, Ruth talked nonstop about her first day, and especially about her new friend, Sue.

"Wonderful!" Mama said. "I'm so glad you have a new friend already. Maybe she can come to our farm and play with you one day soon."

"Yes, thank you, Mama! That would be great! I'd really like to show her my favorite kitten, Boots, and our funny donkey, Ralph."

Ruth had chores to do on the farm and it was her job to feed the smaller animals that lived in the barn. She also helped her older brother, Samuel, clean up the stalls. At times, Daddy let her ride on the tractor with him. Daddy told Ruth she could be anything she wanted to be when she grew up—even a farmer!

Two weeks after school had started, Ruth asked Mama and Daddy if she could have Sue over for playtime.
"It will be fine with us as long as you do your chores before Sue arrives," Daddy said. Then, Mama called Sue's parents to be sure it would be okay for Sue to visit.

On Saturday, Ruth got up even earlier than on a school morning and went outside to feed the animals. Ralph went "hee-haw" as soon as he saw Ruth. Ralph knew he would be taken into the fenced-in field where he could find some apples under the apple tree to eat and run around all day instead of being left in his stall in the barn.

After feeding the other animals, Ruth played with Boots before she went into the kitchen to eat her breakfast.

Meals around the table were a wonderful time for Ruth since the family always ate together and talked about their plans for the day.

"I'm going to have my new school friend, Sue, over for the day," Ruth told Samuel, her brother.

"Well, I'm going to spend the day with Daddy, helping to cut the tall grass in the pasture," Samuel replied.

Farmers call the dried, tall grass "hay." Hay, along with grain, was a source of food for the horse and donkey and also as ground cover in their stalls. Hay was especially helpful for extra warmth during the cold, winter months. The hay was stored in the barn to keep it protected from rain.

Sue and her mother arrived soon after breakfast and Ruth introduced them. Both parents talked awhile before Sue's mother left.

Daddy and Samuel were already in the barn getting the tractor ready so they could begin their work for the day.

Sue lived in town, so she was very excited about going into the barn to see everything. Sue kept telling Ruth how lucky she was to live on a farm and have so many pets to play with every day. Sue loved all the kittens and puppies, but was a little afraid of the ducks and roosters because they were pecking the corn on the ground around her feet. Ruth chased them away when they got too close to Sue. A mouse ran across the barn floor and scared Sue, but the mama cat, Fluffy, quickly chased after it.

Ruth assured Sue that she and her mama did not like mice either: "That's why we always have cats around. Mama cat, Fluffy, is a great mouse hunter!"

While in the barn, they played in a huge pile of fresh hay. Afterward, they were both covered with pieces of hay that clung to their clothes and hair!

After they left the barn, Ruth showed Sue the big pile of corn husks that were left over from harvesting the summer corn crop.

"Gosh! It looks as tall as a mountain!" Sue exclaimed.

"Daddy told me they were going to give the corn husks to a pig farmer down the road," Ruth told Sue. "The dried corn is stored in our big silo and is used as food for the chickens and ducks. Our horse and donkey like the corn, too. What our animals don't need is sold."

The girls went into the field where Ralph, the donkey, was enjoying himself, eating apples.

"Don't try and take an apple out of Ralph's mouth," warned Ruth. "You might get bitten like I did one time."

After showing Sue around the farm, playing with the kittens, and visiting Ralph, the two went into the house to play in Ruth's room. Sue met Ruth's dolls, Margaret and Barbara, and her stuffed rabbit, Harry. Sue laughed when Ruth told her how she and Harry had once gotten all muddy playing outside after a huge rainstorm.

"Mama gave Harry a bath in the washing machine and when the sun came out, Mama hung Harry up by his long ears on the outside clothesline to dry," Ruth told Sue. "Mama threatened to put me into the washer with Harry, too! Of course, she was just teasing. Instead," Ruth said, "I had to take a bath in the middle of the day!"

Before they knew it, it was lunchtime, and Ruth's daddy and brother came in to eat with them. Mama had rung the big brass bell on the front porch to let them know the meal was almost ready. Ruth told Sue that Mama made special lunches for Daddy and Samuel on Saturdays because they were always so hungry after their hard work. Today she had cooked fried chicken, corn on the cob, green beans, made coleslaw, and baked big warm biscuits with butter.

It was all so delicious that everyone cleaned their plates! For dessert, Mama surprised them with a slice of warm apple pie topped with ice cream.

Sue exclaimed, "I've never eaten so much food in my life!"

After lunch, Sue's daddy and brother went back to work in the field and the girls decided to play near the barn with the kittens.

Since Sue did not have a pet, she asked Ruth, "Can I have a kitten to take home?"

Ruth replied, "It would be okay with me, but let's ask Mama anyway."

Mama then called Sue's parents to get their approval. Since they said it would be fine, Sue said, "I'm going to call my new kitten Spot because he has only one white spot."

Sue continued, "I'll keep Spot indoors because there is too much traffic in town and I don't want him to get hurt. I'll use a cardboard box with some old blankets for his bed. I want Spot to sleep right beside me, and when he gets used to his new home, I hope my parents will let him sleep in my bed."

Time passed too fast for the girls and before they knew it, Sue's mom came to take her home. Mama came outside to greet Sue's mother and they talked for awhile.

"Thank you for the wonderful day!" exclaimed Sue. Before they drove away with her new kitten, Spot, Sue said, "Ruth, you are so lucky to live on a farm. I can't wait to visit you again. You will be my best friend forever!"

After they had left, Ruth gave her mama a big hug and said, "Thank you for letting Sue come over and for everything you did to make it a wonderful day! It's so great having Sue as my best friend!"

About the Author

This is Nancy's fourth children's book, which is the sequel to *The Ruth Adventures: Life on the Farm*. Nancy and her husband, Skip, live in Mebane, North Carolina, and are enjoying their "senior years" as parents, grandparents, and even great-grandparents. Nancy enjoys reading, writing, golf, painting, crafts, traveling with Skip, visiting family, church fellowship, spending time with neighbors, and being lazy when time permits. Please look for Nancy's other children's books: *My Nana Was A Free-Range Kid*, *Remembering Joseph Chickadee*, and *The Ruth Adventures: Life on the Farm*. Nancy is presently working on another Ruth book. Nancy would enjoy hearing from you. Her email address is: nancy.p.youngdahl@gmail.com